The Lighthouse Keeper's Rescue

Ronda and David Armitage

ANDRE DEUTSCH

First published in 1989 by
André Deutsch Limited
105–106 Great Russell Street London WC1B 3LJ

British Library Cataloguing in Publication Data

Armitage, Ronda
The lighthouse keeper's rescue
I. Title
823.914 [J]

ISBN 0 233 98428 3

Printed in Hong Kong

Once upon a time there was a lighthouse keeper called Mr Grinling. He lived with Mrs Grinling and their cat, Hamish, in a little white cottage on the cliffs.

Mr Grinling loved his job. He sang as he polished the light; he whistled as he cleaned the windows. But he was especially happy when visitors came. "I'm a lighthouse keeper from my head to my heels," he would tell them cheerfully, "always have been, always will be."

He was also a lighthouse keeper who was getting old. Sometimes he could hear his bones creaking as he climbed the lighthouse stairs. One day Mrs Grinling found him leaning against the shed, sound asleep.

The next day she found him dozing with his head under a heliotrope.

Mrs Grinling woke him gently. "What's the matter, Mr G.?" She asked anxiously. "Are you ill?" "No, Mrs G.," said Mr Grinling, politely. "I'm just having a little snooze in the sun!"

But all was not well. One afternoon Mr Grinling and Hamish rowed out to the lighthouse to prepare the night light. Mr Grinling was rather tired after rowing the dinghy so he decided to have a nap. When he awoke it was quite dark. "Oh those poor boats!" he exclaimed as he rushed into the lighthouse. "I do hope there hasn't been an accident," and he peered anxiously into the darkness.

There hadn't been an accident but somebody had noticed that the light had not come on. A few days later Mr Grinling received a letter from the inspector of lighthouses.

Dear Mr Grinling,
I am very cross. On Monday night your light was an hour late in coming on. This is very dangerous for the ships and boats. If this happens again I shall be extremely angry and FURTHER ACTION will need to be taken.
Yours Faithfully,

For a while Mr Grinling made sure he didn't fall asleep anywhere except in his bed. He didn't lean against shed doors and he didn't rest his head underneath heliotrope flowers.

One sunny afternoon as he was on his way to the lighthouse Mr Grinling stopped to watch two squabbling seagulls.

The dinghy rocked gently up and down. Mr Grinling closed his eyes, leaned back and soon fell fast asleep. The dinghy dipped gently in and out of the waves until it was far beyond the lighthouse.

When the light didn't come on Mrs Grinling began to worry. She rang the coastguard. "Don't fret, love," he shouted down the phone, "I'll send the launch out straight away. We'll soon find him. He's probably gone to sleep again."

But Mr Grinling and Hamish found them first. The crunching
noise as the dinghy hit the launch woke Mr Grinling. For a moment
he was very frightened.

The coastguard shouted down to him. "At last! Hold tight now and we'll give you a tow to the lighthouse. With luck you might get the light on before anybody notices."

But Mr Grinling was not lucky. The next day three inspectors of lighthouses arrived at the little white cottage.

They wore grey suits and long faces. "We are extremely cross, Mr Grinling," they said. "You cannot keep falling asleep, it isn't right for a lighthouse keeper. We must take FURTHER ACTION. You have always been a good and conscientious lighthouse keeper, but now you need to rest. We have given your job to a younger man. Goodbye, Mr Grinling." They shook his hand, took the lighthouse key and left.

Mr Grinling was so upset that he went straight to bed. Nothing that Mrs Grinling did would comfort him. She cooked his favourite breakfast and his favourite dinner. She sang him 'Humpty Dumpty' – his favourite song, but Mr Grinling didn't stir. He just lay there staring at the ceiling.

After a week Mrs Grinling decided she'd had enough. "Mr G.," she said sternly, "I've had enough. You can't lie in bed forever. I need you to help me pack. Now stop this nonsense at once."

So Mr Grinling climbed out of bed and together he and Mrs Grinling packed their trunk. From time to time a tear would roll down Mr Grinling's cheek. "Whatever shall I do, Mrs G.?" he asked sadly. "I'm a lighthouse keeper. I don't know how to be anything else."

They were very tired when they finished the packing, but Mrs Grinling said she wanted a last look through the telescope.

"Whatever's that?" she exclaimed. "There's an enormous black shape on the beach, Mr G. We must find out what it is."

Together they ran down the steep,
winding path to the beach below.

And then they stopped. There it lay on the sand, a great black, shiny whale. "Jiminy Cricket!" exclaimed Mr Grinling. "It's a whale. He must have got lost. We can't leave him here, Mrs G. If he stays out of the water he will die."

"We won't let him die," said Mrs Grinling firmly. "I'll just consult my book." And she did. "We will need help to push him, Mr G.," she decided. "You must ride to the village and bring back as many people as you can find. At 3 o' clock it will be high tide. We might be able to float him then."

"While you're away I shall throw water over him to keep him cool and I shall talk to him so he doesn't feel lonely."

Away went Mr Grinling as fast as his fat little legs could pedal.

All the villagers came. The butcher, the baker and the electrician, the schoolchildren and their teachers, the grannies and the grandads. Some of them ran out of breath and were left behind.

"Hurry!" shouted Mrs Grinling as she saw them coming. "The water's right in now and it's time to push. Everybody gathered round the whale.

"Ready, steady, push," called Mr Grinling. They pushed and shoved and huffed and puffed until everybody was purple in the face. But the whale WAS moving. Slowly the water crept up his big, shiny sides until he was floating.

Everybody stopped pushing and watched.

The whale looked at them, then
with a flick of his enormous black
tail he turned and headed out to
sea. "Goodbye," called the
villagers. "Good luck."

That evening the villagers and the Grinlings watched the whale rescue on the television news.

"It will soon be time for us to say goodbye," said Mrs Grinling. "Tomorrow we have to leave the little white cottage on the cliff. But before we go we'll have a farewell picnic. And we would like you all to come."

Everybody came. The butcher, the baker and the electrician, the children on their bikes and the babies in their pushchairs. It was a very merry affair.

Then three guests turned up, who had not been invited.

"We saw you on the television news," explained the first inspector of lighthouses.
"Yes," said the second inspector, "we were so proud of you and Mrs Grinling."

"We want you to be the lighthouse keeper again," said the third inspector, "but we will give you an assistant. You will work on Mondays, Wednesdays and Fridays and he'll do the rest of the week."

Mr and Mrs Grinling were so delighted that they jumped up and down for joy. "Three cheers for the inspectors of lighthouses," shouted the villagers, "and three cheers for the Grinlings."